Pumpkin Cat

Written & illustrated by Anne Mortimer

KATHERINE TEGEN BOOKS
An Imprint of HarperCollins Publishers

Katherine Tegen Books is an imprint of HarperCollins Publishers.

Pumpkin Cat

Copyright © 2011 by Anne Mortimer

All rights reserved. Manufactured in China.

Library of Congress Cataloging-in-Publication Data

Mortimer, Anne.

Pumpkin cat / written & illustrated by Anne Mortimer. — 1st ed.

p. cm.

Summary: Mouse shows Cat how to grow pumpkins, then turns one into a surprise.
Includes facts about growing pumpkins.

ISBN 978-0-06-187485-7 (trade bdg.) — ISBN 978-0-06-187486-4 (lib. bdg.)

[1. Pumpkin—Fiction. 2. Gardening—Fiction. 3. Cats—Fiction. 4. Mice—Fiction.
5. Halloween—Fiction.] I. Title.

PZ7.M8465Pum 2011   2009049899   [E]—dc22   CIP   AC

Typography by Rachel Zegar

11 12 13 14 15   SCP   10 9 8 7 6 5 4 3 2 1

First Edition

For Ben, Libby, and Molly

One morning in May, Cat wondered,
"How do pumpkins grow?"
"I know," said Mouse.
"And I will show you how."

Cat found some flowerpots.
"What now?" asked Cat.
"Time to add the soil," said Mouse.
So they did.

Cat made holes in the soil with her paws.
"What now?" asked Cat.

"Time to plant the pumpkin seeds," said Mouse.
So they did.

Mouse found a watering can.
"What now?" asked Cat.
"Time to water the seeds," said Mouse.
So they did.

They left the pots in a warm, sunny spot.
Ten days later, two green leaves appeared in each pot.
"What now?" asked Cat.

"Time to plant the seedlings outside," said Mouse.
So they did.

In a few weeks, there were lots of big, prickly leaves and big, yellow, papery flowers covered in pollen.
Lots of bees came and buzzed between the flowers.
"What now?" asked Cat.
"We just watch," said Mouse.
So they did.

By midsummer, each plant had a
fuzzy little green pumpkin.
Caw, caw, caw, called some big crows.

"What now?" asked Cat.
"We need to make a scarecrow," said Mouse.
So they did.

By October, the pumpkins were very big
and very orange.

"What now?" asked Cat.

"Time to pick our pumpkin," said Mouse.

So they did.

"Now," said Mouse, "I am going
to make you a surprise!"

"Happy Halloween!"

Instructions for Growing Pumpkins

1. Plant your pumpkin seeds in early May. Fill small seed pots with good soil and plant two pumpkin seeds in each. Cover the seeds with more soil and water them gently. Leave the pots in a warm, sunny place. Water your plants regularly.

2. In about a week, green leaves should begin to appear. When they do, it is time to plant your young pumpkin seedlings outside in the garden. Be sure that your pumpkins are planted at least fifteen inches apart in a sunny spot. Water your plants when the soil is dry.

3. By July, big, yellow, papery flowers will appear on the pumpkins in your garden. These flowers will last only one day and will be pollinated by the bees. Your job now is just to watch and wait, and remember to keep watering your plants!

4. Next, fuzzy little green pumpkins will appear on your plants. Now you must make a decision: If you want one big pumpkin, you must select one and remove the others. If you leave more than one, your pumpkins will be smaller. Don't forget to keep watering!

5. By October, you'll have orange pumpkins ready to be picked and carved! When you carve your pumpkin, please have an adult help you with the knife. And remember to dry the seeds and save them for next year's pumpkin planting.